ULTIMATE LAMBORGHINI HURACÁN

By Thomas K. Adamson

Kaleidoscope
Minneapolis, MN

The Quest for Discovery Never Ends

···

This edition is co-published by agreement between
Kaleidoscope and World Book, Inc.

Kaleidoscope Publishing, Inc.
6012 Blue Circle Drive
Minnetonka, MN 55343 U.S.A.

World Book, Inc.
180 North LaSalle St., Suite 900
Chicago IL 60601 U.S.A.

All rights reserved. No part of this book may be reproduced in any form without written permission from the publishers.

Kaleidoscope ISBNs
978-1-64519-030-1 (library bound)
978-1-64494-237-6 (paperback)
978-1-64519-130-8 (ebook)

World Book ISBN
978-0-7166-4331-9 (library bound)

Library of Congress Control Number
2019940246

Text copyright ©2020 by Kaleidoscope Publishing, Inc. All-Star Sports, Bigfoot Books, and associated logos are trademarks and/or registered trademarks of Kaleidoscope Publishing, Inc.

Printed in the United States of America.

Bigfoot lurks within one of the images in this book. It's up to you to find him!

TABLE OF CONTENTS

Chapter 1: The Lamborghini Experience 4

Chapter 2: Huracán's History 10

Chapter 3: Eye of the Huracán 16

Chapter 4: Lamborghini Tech 22

    Beyond the Book 28
    Research Ninja 29
    Further Resources 30
    Glossary 31
    Index 32
    Photo Credits 32
    About the Author 32

CHAPTER 1

Huracán is Spanish for hurricane.

THE LAMBORGHINI EXPERIENCE

Ricardo comes to the track. He looks over the Lamborghini Huracán (ur-ah-CAN). He is a pro supercar test driver. But even he is amazed. The car's angry wedge-shaped design looks super cool.

He slides into the driver's seat. He's driven Lamborghinis before. Older Lamborghinis could be hard to drive. Ricardo wonders if the Huracán will have better handling.

He reaches for the start button on the center console. He flips open the red cover. It doesn't really need this cover. But it makes him feel cool. He's in control of something high-powered. Switches and levers cover the dashboard. They make him feel like he's in an airplane.

PARTS OF A
LAMBORGHINI HURACÁN

rear wing

air intakes

Pirelli P Zero Corsa tires

The engine roars to life. He wants to see how fast this car can go.

The car leaps forward. It's going 62 miles per hour (100 km/h). It only took 2.9 seconds. Ricardo wants to test his car's engine and speed. He switches the car to Corsa **mode**. *Corsa* means race. He presses on the gas pedal. The car launches forward. It zooms away with a deafening roar.

wedge shape

Lamborghini logo

Ricardo looks at the speedometer. It says 100 miles per hour (160 km/h). He knows it can go faster. He keeps pushing. The car starts to shake. It reaches 202 miles per hour (325 km/h)!

The engine growls loudly. It sounds amazing. It shifts smoothly between gears. Ricardo's heart races. He turns a corner. The car turns quickly. The Huracán is easier to steer than older models. Ricardo is pleased.

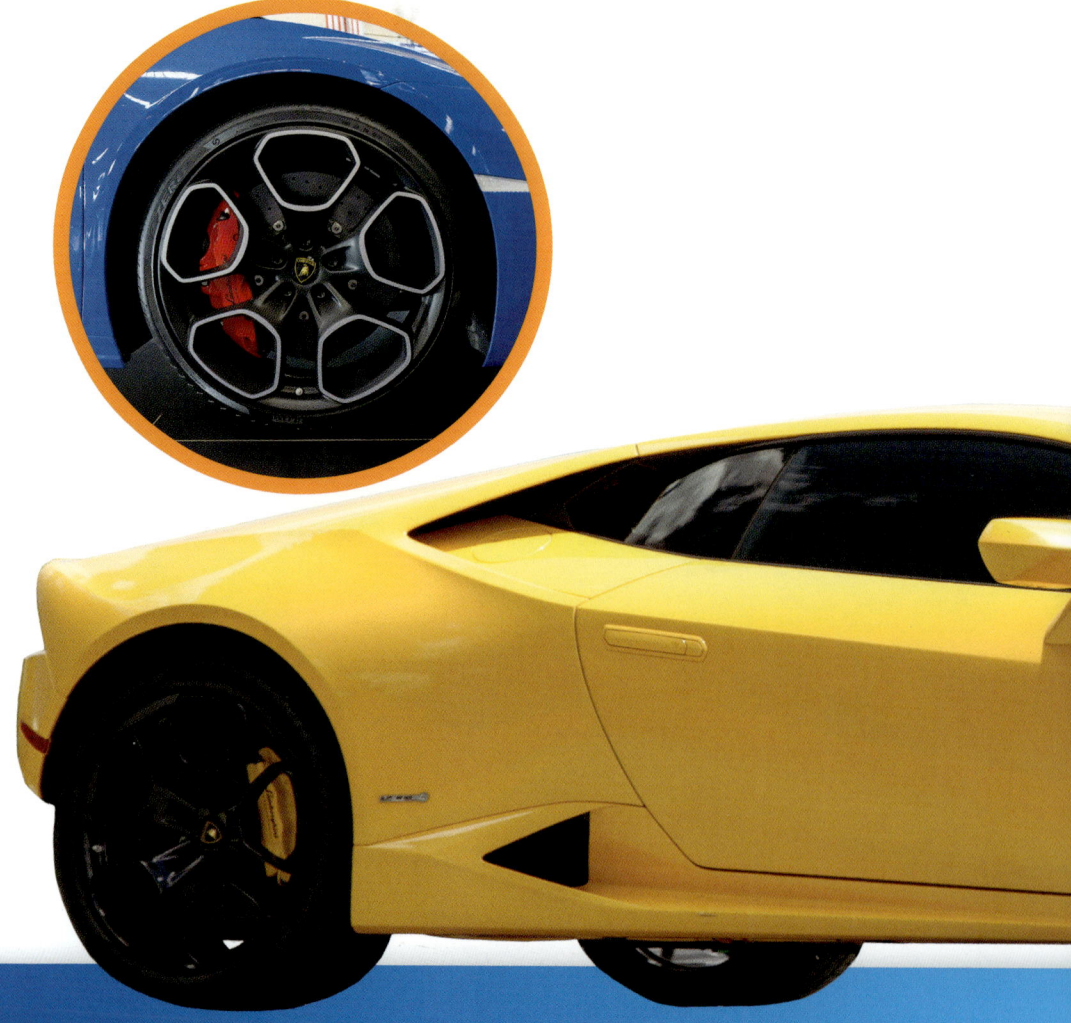

The colors of the Italian flag appear on the Huracán Performante.

The Lamborghini Huracán has a top speed of 202 miles per hour (325 km/h).

FUN FACT
Lamborghini fans can "visit" the Lamborghini museum on Google Street View.

CHAPTER 2

HURACÁN'S HISTORY

It's the 1960s in Italy. Ferruccio Lamborghini is a successful man. He owns a tractor company near Bologna. He wants to show off his wealth. He buys a Ferrari. These are the best sports cars around. But Lamborghini isn't impressed with his Ferrari. He has trouble with the **clutch**. He decides to replace it. Lamborghini takes the car apart. But he discovers something shocking. The clutch is the same kind used in his tractors! But he paid a lot more for his Ferrari's clutch. Lamborghini tells Enzo Ferrari this.

That makes Ferrari mad. Ferrari says Lamborghini is just a tractor driver. Lamborghini is furious. But he is inspired. In 1963, he starts his own sports car company. He wants to make cars better than Ferraris.

The Lamborghini company became famous. It made supercars that looked like none other. The cars were sporty. They were low to the ground. But many people considered them difficult to drive. The ride was rough. They could be hard to steer.

Lamborghinis always had a unique look. People marveled at their futuristic designs.

Lamborghini makes GT racing versions of the Huracán.

Things changed in 1998. The car company Audi took over Lamborghini. Audi worked on making Lamborghinis better. Engineers knew the cars still needed to look **stylish**. Lamborghini fans already liked the way the cars looked. Audi needed to make buyers want to drive one.

So the engineers worked more on the driving experience. Driving a Lamborghini had to be memorable. They wanted to improve the handling. They made the next Lamborghini even more powerful.

Audi's first Lamborghini model came in 2001. It was the Murciélago. The Gallardo came in 2003. These cars were very successful. Owners loved showing them off. They still looked super cool. But now they were fun to drive. The Gallardo became Lamborghini's most successful car.

Where the Huracán Is Made

1. **Sant'Agata Bolognese, Italy:** Lamborghini headquarters; Lamborghini factory, where Lamborghini Huracáns are assembled

2. **Győr, Hungary:** Audi factory, where Lamborghini engines are built

The great minds at Lamborghini didn't stop there. Car makers have to keep finding new ideas. They find ways to make cars even better. They then created the Huracán. It replaced the Gallardo.

The first Huracán was a **coupe**. It was made in 2014. The Huracán Spyder is a **convertible**. It was first made in 2016. The Performante was introduced in 2017. It was the fastest Huracán yet. The EVO was the next Huracán model. This model added more technology.

FUN FACT
Lamborghini chose a bull for its logo because his zodiac sign is Taurus the bull.

THE FIGHTING BULL

"Huracán" is the name of a Spanish fighting bull. This bull was famous in 1879. It was known for its courage. Many Lamborghini models are named for famous fighting bulls. Lamborghini's logo is a charging bull.

The Huracán Spyder's top folds up in 17 seconds.

CHAPTER 3

EYE OF THE HURACÁN

Antonio walks into the Lamborghini dealership. He's heard good things about the Huracán. He is thinking of adding it to his collection.

"Can you tell me about the Huracán?" Antonio asks a salesperson.

She leads him to a Huracán on display. It's metallic red. It has black wheels. It looks amazing.

FUN FACT
The grilles, door handles, air vents, and gas cap all feature hexagons.

"This is the Performante," the salesperson says. "It's the fastest model. The Huracán has three driving modes. They are Strada, Sport, and Corsa. *Strada* means street. This mode is for everyday driving. It offers the most comfortable ride."

There are three models of Huracán. Each model has a coupe and convertible version.

She opens the door. Antonio looks inside.

"Do you see this red switch? This changes the driving mode. Sport mode makes the engine more aggressive. This can be for high speed. It can also climb a mountain road. *Corsa* means race. The **suspension system** becomes stiffer. This makes the steering response quicker. Corsa mode makes the ride too rough for street driving. It's just for fun on the test track."

FUN FACT
In Sport and Corsa modes, the engine is even louder than usual!

The controls for driving mode, turn signals, and windshield wipers are all on the steering wheel.

"That sounds like a lot of fun," Antonio says.

"The Huracán has a **V10** engine," the salesperson says. She leads him to the back of the car. Antonio can see the engine. It's covered with glass.

THE HURACÁN PERFORMANTE
IN DETAIL

Height: 3.8 feet (1.2 m)

Width: 7.3 feet (2.2 m)

- Length: 14.8 feet (4.5 m)
- Weight: 3,047 pounds (1,382 kg)
- Top Speed: 202 miles per hour (325 km/h)
- Time from 0–62 miles per hour (0–100 km/h): 2.9 seconds

COST: $282,885

"Our engineers worked hard on the Huracán's design. Its **aerodynamic** system has two parts. It has a front **spoiler**. There's also a rear wing. The rear wing helps it stick to the road. This makes it super quick when driving around corners."

Antonio loves the car. "What is it made out of?"

"The car's body is made of **carbon fiber** and aluminum. These are light materials. A lighter car is a faster car. Carbon fiber is extra strong."

Antonio sits inside the car. He puts his hands on the wheel. He imagines speeding around a racetrack.

"Would you like to take it for a test drive?"

Antonio smiled. This was going to be exciting.

Only the Huracán Performante has a rear wing.

CHAPTER 4

LAMBORGHINI TECH

Rachel ran to the mailbox. Her favorite magazine was arriving today. This issue was special. It had an article about the Huracán.

She went up to her room. She had Lamborghini posters on the wall. Toy Lamborghinis sat on her shelf. She hoped to own a Lamborghini one day.

Rachel admired the Huracán on the cover. It was bright green. She opened the magazine. The EVO was the newest Huracán model. It was released in 2019. The article said the EVO was the best Huracán yet. It added more luxury. It was even easier to drive.

The Huracán EVO was released in 2019.

The EVO had a smarter computer. It adjusted driving modes to what the driver needed. A new touch screen on the console was easy to use. It controlled the music and the maps. The article said there was another cool feature. There were lights inside the car. They changed color with the driving mode. Rachel was impressed. She kept reading.

A spoiler on the front created more airflow under the car. The EVO had four-wheel steering. This made taking corners easier and faster. Even drivers who weren't pro racers could drift around corners!

FUN FACT
The interior lights are blue in Strada, yellow in Sport, and red in Corsa.

People all over the world drive Lamborghinis.

Lamborghini will continue to make fast, stylish cars for years to come.

The article didn't just talk about the EVO. It said Lamborghini was working on an all-electric supercar. The Terzo Millennio would not use gas. This name means "Third Millennium" in Italian. Now that's really looking to the future.

Rachel couldn't wait to see what the future would hold. Lamborghini would continue to innovate. Their cars would look amazing. They would also have the newest technology. Lamborghinis would be fun to drive for years to come. She couldn't wait until she was old enough to drive one!

THE POPE'S HURACÁN

In 2017, Lamborghini gave a Huracán to Pope Francis. It was one of a kind. It was white with yellow stripes. Pope Francis signed it. The car sold for $860,000 at an auction. The money was donated to charity.

BEYOND
THE BOOK

After reading the book, it's time to think about what you learned. Try the following exercises to jumpstart your ideas.

THINK

THAT'S NEWS TO ME. The Huracán EVO came out in 2019. How might news sources be able to fill in more detail about this? What new information could you find in news articles? Where could you go to find those sources?

CREATE

PRIMARY SOURCES. A primary source is an original document, photograph, or interview. Make a list of different primary sources you might be able to find about the Huracán. What new information might you learn from these sources?

SHARE

WHAT'S YOUR OPINION? This book claims that the EVO is the best Huracán model. Do you agree or disagree with this position? Use evidence from the text to support your answer. Share your position and evidence with a friend. Does your friend agree with you?

GROW

REAL-LIFE RESEARCH. What places could you visit to learn more about the Lamborghini Huracán? What other things could you learn while you were there?

RESEARCH NINJA

Visit www.ninjaresearcher.com/0301 to learn how to take your research skills and book report writing to the next level!

RESEARCH

DIGITAL LITERACY TOOLS

SEARCH LIKE A PRO
Learn about how to use search engines to find useful websites.

FACT OR FAKE?
Discover how you can tell a trusted website from an untrustworthy resource.

TEXT DETECTIVE
Explore how to zero in on the information you need most.

SHOW YOUR WORK
Research responsibly—learn how to cite sources.

WRITE

GET TO THE POINT
Learn how to express your main ideas.

PLAN OF ATTACK
Learn prewriting exercises and create an outline.

DOWNLOADABLE REPORT FORMS

FURTHER RESOURCES

BOOKS

Crum, Colin. *Ferrari vs. Lamborghini*. Windmill Books, 2014.

Cruz, Calvin. *Lamborghini Aventador*. Bellwether Media, 2016.

Kingston, Seth. *The History of Lamborghinis*. PowerKids Press, 2019.

WEBSITES

Factsurfer.com gives you a safe, fun way to find more information.

1. Go to www.factsurfer.com.
2. Enter "Lamborghini Huracán" into the search box and click 🔍.
3. Select your book cover to see a list of related websites.

GLOSSARY

aerodynamic: An aerodynamic design reduces the drag, or pull, on a car as it moves through air. The Lamborghini Huracán has an aerodynamic system to help the car move faster.

carbon fiber: Carbon fiber is a very strong, lightweight material. Using carbon fiber to build a car makes it lighter and faster.

clutch: The clutch of a car helps the driver shift gears. Lamborghini was mad when he realized he paid lots of money for the same clutch that was in his tractors.

convertible: A car with a top that can be put down is a convertible. The Huracán Spyder convertible has a top that folds back.

coupe: A car with two doors is called a coupe. A coupe usually only has enough room for two people.

mode: A mode is a way of doing something. Corsa is a driving mode on the Lamborghini Huracán.

spoiler: A spoiler is a flat piece on the back or front of a car to give the car better handling. To create downforce and improve a car's handling, a spoiler is added to many supercars.

stylish: Something that is stylish displays the latest style or fashion. People like that Lamborghinis look so stylish.

suspension system: A car's suspension system gives the car a smooth ride over bumps. The Lamborghini's suspension system is extra stiff in Corsa mode.

V10: A V10 engine has ten cylinders in the shape of a V. A Lamborghini Huracán has a V10 gas engine.

INDEX

Audi, 12

bulls, 14, 15

Corsa mode, 7, 17–18, 19
cost, 20

dashboard, 5, 18

engine, 7–8, 19
EVO, 14, 23–27

Ferrari, Enzo, 10–11
Francis (pope), 27

Gallardo, 12–14

Italy, 10–11, 13

Lamborghini, Ferruccio, 10–11
logo, 7, 14, 15

museum, 9

Performante, 14, 16–21

rear wing, 6, 21

size, 20
steering, 8, 11, 25
style, 5, 12, 16, 27

Terzo Millennio, 27
top speed, 8, 20

PHOTO CREDITS

The images in this book are reproduced through the courtesy of: Ilyshev Dmitry/Shutterstock Images, front cover (desert); Lamborghini Media Center, front cover (car); Dong liu/Shutterstock Images, p. 3; Christopher Lyzcen/Shutterstock Images, p. 4; Nameez/Shutterstock Images, pp. 4–5; Chatchai Somwat/Shutterstock Images, pp. 6–7; mrfiza/Shutterstock Images, p. 8; tomeng/iStockphoto, pp. 8–9; Zavatskiy Aleksandr/Shutterstock Images, p. 9; Chekunov/Shutterstock Images, pp. 10–11; Dan74/Shutterstock Images, p. 12; Red Line Editorial, p. 13; cristian ghisla/Shutterstock Images, pp. 14–15; Foto by M/Shutterstock Images, pp. 16–17; Sjo/iStockphoto, pp. 18–19; worachat/Shutterstock Images, p. 20; eans/Shutterstock Images, p. 21; Pix4Pix/Shutterstock Images, p. 22; Grzegorz Czapski/Shutterstock Images, pp. 22–23; Art Konovalov/Shutterstock Images, pp. 24–25; i viewfinder/Shutterstock Images, pp. 26–27; L'Osservatore Romano/AP Images, p. 27; David Prince/Shutterstock Images, p. 30.

ABOUT THE AUTHOR

Thomas K. Adamson has written dozens of nonfiction books for kids on sports, space, history, math, cool vehicles, and more. He enjoys sports, card games, reading and playing ball with his two sons, and playing with his Morkie named Moe.